THE FANTASTIC FLATULENT
FART BROTHERS

SAVE THE
WORLD!

by M.D. Whalen

illustrated by Des Campbell

This is a work of fiction. Names, characters, places, and incidents are either products of the author's imagination or, if real, are used fictitiously.

First US edition, published 2017

Top Floor Books
imprint of stvdio media
PO Box 29
Silvermine Bay, Hong Kong

visit us at www.topfloorbooks.com

ISBN 978 962 7866 27 5

CONTENTS

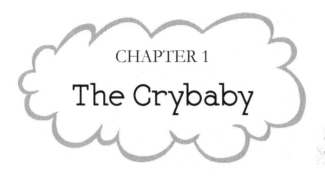

CHAPTER 1
The Crybaby

Meet Willy. He likes to lie around eating chips and nose goo. He also cries at TV commercials.

"No, I don't," Willy said.

Sure he does. When the girl in the shampoo commercial woke up with hair as tangled as a puked-up cat hairball, making her embarrassed to go to school, it was the saddest thing he had ever seen.

Willy's eyes welled up.

"I will not cry," he said. "I...will...not..."

Oh no! Here comes the girl's mother!

Tears spilled down Willy's cheeks and onto the sofa. He wiped snot from his nose, then sucked it off his fingers. It was stretchy, with lumpy, chewable bits, which cheered him up a little.

The girl's mother held up a shampoo bottle and smiled. No mother smiled like that in real life! Willy couldn't bear to watch. *Get out, girl! Run!*

The front door banged open. It was Willy's big brother Peter.

"Hey, guess what? I just farted up a school bus full of Girl Scouts!"

Peter pointed his butt at Willy. "First I gave 'em a Stealth Stinker, like this."

pffffooOOOIT!

A smile struggled to break through Willy's trembling lips.

"Some were still standing, so I let out a Drone Attacker."

BRRRRUMMFF-FF-FF-FF-ffffff...!

"When the driver pulled over to grab me, I gave him a full Foghorn Blast right in the face and escaped."

Peter sure knew how to cheer up a guy. Willy turned over on the sofa and farted a loud one straight at his brother. Then they both tumbled onto the floor, kicking their feet and laughing so hard that Willy choked on the last mucus dribbling over his lip. Who cared anymore about a stupid shampoo girl?

But speaking of girls...

Their little sister Skyler skipped into the living room, hugging a doll and a blankie.

"Ew! I heard you guys. You're gross!"

"Oh yeah?" Peter said. "You haven't seen gross."

HONNNNNNNK-popple-popple-SPLEEP!

He let out a green, greasy cloud that stunk like prehistoric rotten eggs.

Skyler snuffled. Her face went red. She squeezed her fists at her sides. A major tantrum was about to erupt. Which meant Willy and Peter were in deep trouble.

Last time Skyler threw a tantrum, they'd had to do laundry duty and not only touch their sister's undies, but put them away in her icky-girlie underwear drawer!

Willy made a funny face, just in time.

Skyler relaxed and said, "So what

are you getting me for my birthday on Monday?"

Willy and Peter looked at each other. They'd forgotten their sister's birthday, just three days from now.

Just then a news bulletin came on TV:

"Breaking news! The Yummy Tummy Onion Dip Factory, world's largest maker of onion dip, has been destroyed in a huge explosion. Panic buying has emptied store shelves of onion dip, causing a world-wide shortage. The Wize Krakker Evil Clown Corps is claiming responsibility for the attack."

"Aah! That's the worst news ever!" Peter said.

"What? Some dumb dip factory?" Skyler said.

"No. I mean your birthday coming up." Peter tooted out a little fart and laughed.

"Gross!! You're the worst brothers in the whole wide world!"

Skyler ran crying out of the room.

"Now you did it, dummy," Willy said. "Now we have to get her a real present or we're dead meat, folding undies forever... or worse: girls' pajama bottoms."

"Shh! Look!" Peter said.

Another TV commercial came on.

"Whoopee! It's the Death Breeze 3000, the most futuristic whoopee cushion ever made, brought to you by the Roadapple Corporation."

"Cutting edge—get it? Cutting?—new *Flatulatronics technology lets you make the grossest, spewiest, splatteringest, stomach-turning, ear-twisting noises such as the world has never heard before.*

"*But that's not all! Our unique, patented i-Stink mode transmits eighteen different stinky stenches, smellable up to half a mile away.*

"*Get down to your local toy store today! Be first to own the smelly new—**PFLLLL-KATHWORPPP!**—Oops! Har har!—Death Breeze 3000!*"

Peter sprang up. "That's it!"

"What's it?" Will said.

Peter grabbed Willy and dragged him out the door, while humming a birthday song.

CHAPTER 2
Plane Full of Nuns

Willy had a hard time keeping up as he and Peter ran the fourteen blocks to the toy store. He caught his breath at a stoplight, and said, "You're not really thinking of getting Skyler one of those whoopee cushions for her birthday? Girls don't like that stuff."

"It's not just a whoopee cushion, it's the Death Breeze 3000. Of course she'll like it. Everyone in the world's going to want one!"

On that last point, Peter was right. The line from the toy store stretched three blocks and moved at the pace of a snail's grandfather. Not even Peter's sourest, gassiest farts made people leave. That trick didn't work in this crowd!

Finally, they were inside. The prize was in sight. The kid in front of Willy and Peter bought two Death Breeze 3000's and danced away. Peter held out money between his trembling fingers. But the saleswoman said, "Sorry," and put up a sign: **SOLD OUT**

"No! It can't be!" Peter shrieked. Kids holding bought-and-paid-for Death Breeze 3000's stuck their tongues out at him.

The saleswoman said, "Come back next week."

"But our sister's birthday is Monday," Peter pleaded.

"Wish I could help you gentlemen," the sales woman said.

"I know," Peter said. "Maybe call another branch of your store, and ask them to hold one for us."

The saleswoman went to her office to call. Willy walked to a shelf and picked up a blue pony doll with pink hair. Squeezing it made an adorable little "Neee" sound. Now, *this* was what girls liked. "Let's get her a My Cutie Horsie," he said.

Peter scowled.

"Just get it over with," Willy said.

"Anyway, she'll like it and maybe leave us alone."

Peter didn't say anything as Willy placed the blue pony on the sales counter.

Just then a kid walked past with a Death Breeze 3000 in a shopping bag and blew them a loud razzie. Peter's face went red. He swept the My Cutie Horsie onto the floor. "This has become a matter of family honor. How will we look to the rest of the neighborhood if we're the only home without a Death Breeze 3000?"

The saleswoman returned, shaking her head. "Seems we're sold out almost everywhere. The closest place with a Death Breeze 3000 in stock is our South Beantown branch."

"Beantown? Isn't that on the other side of the country?" Peter said.

"Got that right," the saleswoman said.

Willy tried to tug his brother toward

the My Cutie Horsies. Maybe he'd go for the purple one with orange hair. But Peter pulled his arm free and announced to the saleswoman: "Tell them to hold it for us!"

"How are we supposed to get to Beantown?" Willy said.

Peter pointed to the corner bus stop, where a sign said *Airport bus.* "We can fly there and be back in time for dinner."

"How are we supposed to pay for plane tickets?"

"You hungry? I am," Peter said.

"What's that got to do with plane tickets?"

"You'll see."

Peter led them to a supermarket across the street, where they bought bags and bags of cheese-and-garlic potato chips and a whole carton of canned bean dip.

Once they were on the bus, Peter said, "Start eating."

By the time they reached the airport, Willy felt like a balloon ready to burst. Peter stood on one side of the entrance gate and Willy on the other. When the flight was announced, Peter gave a thumbs-up. They both leaned over and exploded out massive, suffocating stink clouds.

The lined-up passengers choked. They retched. They shouted, "Eww!" The fart clouds swirled together around the ticket taker, who fainted onto the floor. Peter and Willy dashed through the gate and straight onto the plane.

Half the seats on board were filled with black-robed nuns. An evil grin crept across Peter's face.

"Um, maybe we should keep a low profile," Willy said, shrinking into his seat.

"And lose the chance of a lifetime?"

The plane took off. Willy and Peter watched cartoons and stuffed themselves on airline cabbage-and-onion sandwiches and orange soda.

Willy's stomach gurgled. Peter's bubbled.

They jumped up and down to shake everything up inside them. This was a truly bad idea, Willy thought. But a truly funny one.

Willy's guts fizzed and frothed. Peter's poppled and plopped.

They bent over in the aisle. Out foamed thick clouds of rotten stink that smelled like the innards of a thousand garbage trucks. The air turned green; the nuns' faces turned greener. Veils popped off gagging heads.

Peter and Willy held their bellies, laughing and laughing, rolling side to side on the floor.

Or was it the airplane rolling and rocking?

People screamed. People fainted. The pilot staggered out of the cockpit, clasping an oxygen mask to his face. "Who did this?"

Everyone pointed. That is, everyone who was still able to breathe.

"Aaaahhhhh!!!" said Willy and Peter.

CHAPTER 3

Lost at Sea

Willy and Peter floated in the middle of a wide ocean, no land in sight. Not even a bird flew overhead. The sun burned their heads. All they had to hold onto were their cartons of chips and dip.

Willy cried and blubbered. His nose ran with snot, which didn't taste half bad, actually, after all those airline sandwiches.

"What are we gonna do? I can't swim good. And I'm scared of sharks!"

His tears flowed so hard the sea rose three full inches. Or maybe that was just a passing sea swell.

"We still got our potato chips," Peter said.

"I don't care about potato chips! I want to go home!" Willy cried even harder and the sea rose some more. Gray clouds gathered on the horizon.

"I mean those bags are full of air. If we

tie them together we can make a raft," Peter said. "Hand me your shoelaces."

In a little while they were bobbing on their potato chip raft. But those clouds were coming closer, and they were dark and looked a bit mean. A storm would be bad news on the open sea. They didn't even have an umbrella.

Peter grabbed a passing stick. "Give me your shirt!" he said. He tied their shirts together into a makeshift sail.

"By my calculation, we should head west," Peter said. He shaded his eyes and looked toward the sun. "You're better at science. The sun rises in the west, right?"

"I'm pretty sure it rises in the east," Willy said.

"West."

"East."

"West, you idiot!"

"East, you dumb-butt!"

Maybe it was the heat and the salt in his eyes, but Willy couldn't take any more. He raised his fists, and Peter did the same. Just then they heard rumbling like a gassy stomach, though it wasn't either of theirs.

Lightning flashed. The dark clouds were closer and scarier than ever.

"We can't panic," Willy said. "When people disagree, what's the democratic thing to do? We compromise!"

"Good idea. Let's go that way instead." Peter pointed south. Or was it north?

But no matter which way they pointed, there wasn't enough wind.

Peter grabbed cans of bean dip from the carton. "Eat!"

They ate. And ate. And ate. Until the rumbling in their bellies was louder than the approaching storm—though without the lightning shooting from the ever-angrier clouds.

They got on their knees and dropped their pants, but held it in until Willy felt like knives pierced his gut.

Finally, Peter said, "Now." They aimed the sharpest, squealiest, strongest stink jets of their lives straight at the sail.

It was kind of fun the way they practically flew over the swells. At the top of one wave, Willy saw a sight so welcome he nearly lost control of his butt. "Land ho!"

A rocky island dipped and rolled into view while behind them the sky turned nearly black. The sea boiled.

"Turn up the juice!" Peter shouted.

They gulped bean dip down to one last can. Willy's butt was on fire, but he couldn't lose control now. He aimed the malodorous air stream in a focused, powerful flow.

Lightning crashed so close, one of the raft's bags burst, ridged potato chips flying everywhere. Peter cracked open the last can of dip. The took turns licking it clean. Then Willy and Peter locked eyes and nodded to one another. This was it. Their lives depended on one last fart.

"Ready..."

"Aim..."

Willy let go until he thought he'd blown out every molecule from inside his body.

The raft shot skyward. Lightning struck left and right, ahead and behind.

"Aaaahhhhhh!!!" said Willy and Peter for the second time that day.

They crashed down hard, potato chip bags bursting beneath their bodies, and tumbled across wet white sand. Rain pelted down, stinging their faces.

Willy pointed to an opening in a rocky cliff. "A cave!"

Inside it was dry and warm. Crabs scuttled aside. The boys lay on their backs and caught their breath, then gave each other a high five.

"We did it! We're safe!" Willy said.

"Of course. We're the coolest, smartest, strongest guys in the universe. Nothing can ever harm us!" Peter said.

An ugly laugh echoed behind them, like the squish of a plunger clearing a blocked toilet.

"What have we here?" said a deep, scratchy voice coming from an evil clown face, grinning through red dripping teeth.

"Aaaahhhhhh!!!" said Willy and Peter for the third time.

CHAPTER 4

Balloon Dilemma

The clown croaked out a long, gurgling belch, then laughed again.

"Care for some strawberry soda?" That might explain the red teeth.

"Um...sure," Willy said. He was pretty thirsty after all that bean dip and potato chips and sea water, not to mention the boogers he'd been treating himself to when Peter wasn't looking.

A liquid jet shot from a flower on the clown's chest, drenching Willy and Peter in sticky, sweet soda pop.

Peter waved a fist. "Not funny, you stupid clown!"

The strange thing was, the clown seemed to agree. He didn't even crack a smile.

"I do apologize," the clown said. "Allow me to introduce myself. Kookie the Clown at your service." He bowed and lifted his little derby hat. A boxing glove sprang out and knocked Peter to the ground.

Then he turned his attention to Willy.

Willy wanted to run away, but his path was blocked by the evil Kookie. He swallowed hard, trying not to cry.

"Where are we?" Willy said.

"You really don't know? This is Wize Krakker Island. Lots of kids come here."

Willy looked at Peter. They'd heard that name before.

"Aren't you the ones who blew up the onion dip factory?" Peter said.

Kookie the Clown put on a huge grin. He was nuts. "Wanna see a balloon act?"

Did they have a choice?

Kookie pulled a fistful of colored balloons from his pocket and blew up a long, skinny one, then another and another, all the while making *ha-ha* and *hee-haw* noises, though they sure didn't sound funny to Willy's ears.

The clown twisted balloons into loops and hooks, which didn't look like any balloon animal Willy had ever seen. In fact, they looked more like...

Chains.

Kookie threw back his head and shook with squishy laughter, while he looped the chains around Willy and Peter, trapping them inside multi-colored balloon cocoons.

For the fourth time that day, Willy and Peter said, *"Aaaahhhhhh!!!"*

CHAPTER 5
Stinky Beasts

Kookie the Clown looped one last balloon around Willy and Peter, and dragged them across the cave's sandy floor. Willy tried to squirm free, but the harder he struggled, the tighter the balloons became.

If only that dumb Peter had listened and bought the My Cutie Horsie, they wouldn't have ended up lost at sea, nearly fried by lightning, and now, dragged through dirt by an evil, crazy clown.

He was about to say something angry, when Peter exclaimed, "If only that dumb Skyler hadn't asked for a birthday present!"

Of course, Willy thought. He'd almost forgotten the Rule of Little Brotherhood:

When all else fails, blame your sister.

Kookie pulled them toward an opening in the side of the cave. Bright sunlight seared Willy's eyes.

Something outside was chewing  really loud, then, with a huge, wet *ka-TOOEY,* a spit wad the size of a baseball struck him in the chest. Well, luckily it struck his balloon bindings and slid right off.

Willy was face-to-face with a camel. Not just one, but three!

Strong hands lifted Willy onto one animal's back, and Peter onto another. A word from Kookie, and the camels began to move, rocking Willy up and down and side to side. He tried hard not to cry, but a tear dribbled down his cheek. Worse, with both hands tied down by balloons, he wasn't able to clear the creamy snot from his nose.

"Where are you taking us?" Peter said, more angry than scared.

Kookie, behind them on the third camel, said, "You'll smell it when we get there," and finished with his ugly, squishy laugh.

They rode for hours across a pale, rocky landscape. Willy had heard of desert islands, but this one really was a desert. He'd never felt so uncomfortable, bouncing on a hairy back, encased in balloons under a blazing hot sun.

At last, they stopped in the shade of a huge boulder. Kookie squirted strawberry soda into Willy's and Peter's mouths, then spread food on the ground for the camels.

"We're hungry too, you idiot!" Peter shouted. "And sweaty and itchy under these stupid balloons!"

Kookie's evil clown face looked up with an evil grin. Reaching into his evil hat, he pulled out an evil-looking hat pin the size of a Chinese chopstick. Then he rushed at Peter like an evil clown swordsman.

Willy couldn't look, partly because he was crying.

A loud burst, then another. The clown stood beside Peter, popping balloons and laughing. Soon Peter was free.

It was Willy's turn next. He nearly wet his pants while colored rubber spattered around him. What a relief to move his arms again, but watching the camels eat made his stomach growl.

"What about us? We're hungry," he said.

"You'll eat when we get there," Kookie said. "Onward ho!"

Bouncing on the camel again made Willy's hunger worse. He felt inside his nose, but it had nothing to offer.

When Kookie wasn't looking, he reached into the camel food bag strung over the animal's side, and shoved a handful into his mouth. It tasted awful, like dry weeds and mud. But at least it gave his stomach something to do.

Just then his camel's body rumbled and trembled like an earthquake he could feel through his legs. A long, violent buzz filled his ears like a power lawnmower.

His camel lurched forward.

"Ewwwww!" Peter shouted from behind.

Willy turned around. Peter's face turned from green to yellow to purple to white. The air around him shimmered.

"That was the longest, loudest, grossest, stinkiest fart in the entire history of fartitude," Peter shouted with joy in his voice.

Then his own camel cut an even bigger, longer, louder fart. But was it stinkier?

Riding behind them, Kookie the Clown's white makeup changed to light green, his eyes bugged out, lips crunched together and he swooned side to side, nearly falling off his mount.

Yes, definitely stinkier.

It wasn't long before Willy's own insides started to tremble. His belly felt like it was full of lava boiling and bubbling just before a volcanic eruption.

Which was a pretty good comparison, because moments later, a gas jet spewed from his butt with an ear-twisting *BLRRRRRRRRRRRPPP,* so hard and long and loud and gross that his camel lurched forward like a turbo-powered race car.

"Ewwwww!" Peter shouted from behind. His face again went green, then yellow, then purple. "What did you eat?"

"Just some camel food."

"Whoa!" Peter said. "I gotta try some!"

The brothers spent the rest of the journey competing to make the biggest, greasiest, ugliest-sounding camel food farts.

They were a bit disappointed when they reached the foot of the mountain, and Kookie announced: "Play time's over."

Leaving the camels behind, they marched up a steep, narrow path to a heavy wooden gate. Kookie honked an old-fashioned bicycle horn hanging outside.

After a short wait, the door squealed open and a red clown nose emerged.

"A couple more for you," Kookie said.

A pair of mean-looking clowns dragged Peter and Willy inside, and sealed the door behind them with a massive iron bolt. Then they hurled the boys through the air.

"Aaaahhhhhh!!!" How many times was that today? Willy had lost count.

Somewhere deep inside the rock, a crazy laugh echoed back.

"Hoo hee ha ha walla walla wing ding!"

CHAPTER 6
Unfunny Farts

Willy came down hard. But instead of breaking every bone in his body... *he bounced up.*

Then hit the floor and bounced again.

Peter dropped beside him, springing up and down like a basketball.

"This whole place is a big, stupid, babyish bouncy castle," Peter said.

"Hoo hee ha ha walla walla wing ding!"

That laugh again!

It came from a red inflatable throne in

the middle of the room.

The weirdest, evilest clown Willy had ever seen peered down at them.

Purple hair puffed out like weeds from the sides of a white egg-shaped head. His face was covered in bright-colored tattoos: bats swirling across each cheek, leaving trails of puffy green clouds, while a dragon shot fire across the forehead... only the flame came not from its mouth but from its green and orange butt.

The clown's thick red slug-like lips smiled, revealing teeth painted in a rainbow of colors.

"Welcome home," it said in a squeaky clown voice.

"Wh-what do you mean?" Willy said.

"Because once you enter this door, you never, ever leave! *Hoo hee ha ha walla walla wing ding!*"

The clown's eyes rolled in circles, while

his head wagged side to side, laughing like a broken cuckoo clock.

"What are we doing here? Why can't we leave?" Peter demanded. "Who are you?"

"So many questions!" the clown said. "Though sadly, not the right ones, nor in the right order. Ah, but you must be thirsty after your long journey."

Not again, Willy thought. He tilted his head so nothing would squirt in his eyes.

Splash!

Sticky liquid poured onto his upturned face: grape soda this time. Way overhead, a clown on a swing emptied a bucket over him and Peter.

Tattoo-face leaned forward, the bouncy castle throne wiggling around him. "Welcome, my young friends. I'm Booby the Clown. Yes, *the* Booby the Clown. Here's my card."

A little card spun through the air and landed at Willy's knees.

Willy tucked it in his shirt pocket.

"Haven't you heard of me?" Booby the Clown said. "No, I can see by your faces you haven't. Alas! Nobody's heard of me, not in years and years!"

He pressed his hand to his forehead in a fake dramatic pose.

"And that's why you're here. To make sure the whole world never again forgets my name. You, my lucky young gentlemen, will assist me in becoming President of Our Planet in Eternity. *Hoo hee ha ha walla walla wing ding!*"

His cuckoo clock laugh echoed off the rubbery walls.

Willy had to admit he was a teeny

bit scared. He blinked back tears, but couldn't control his other end. His insides still rumbled from all that camel food. His butt whistled a stinky little *fff-thweeeee*. Peter snort-laughed.

Booby the Clown stood up on his seat. "Guards!"

Two clowns rushed in. One shoved a giant cork into Peter's mouth.

"Farts are not funny!" Booby the Clown jumped up and down on his bouncy throne, waving his fists. "Did you hear me? *Farts! Are! Not! Funny!*"

The other clown guard grabbed Willy and another giant cork, but instead of Willy's mouth, it seemed to be aimed at his bottom.

"Wait!" Willy shouted. "I'm—I'm—I'm s-s-sorry to d-disagree...uh...sir. But most people think farts are kind of funny."

Booby the Clown leapt from the

throne, plopping down so close to Willy their noses nearly touched. Long, white-gloved fingers pinched Willy's chin. The clown's breath smelled like a baloney and mayonnaise sandwich.

"Is that so, my little friend? Can you explain to me why farts are funny?"

Willy tried to shake his head, but it was caught in the clown's grip.

"No? Come now, try," Booby said. "Still can't explain why they're funny? Do you know why? *Because they're not! They're disgusting. They're dirty. They're cheap!* By the time I'm finished putting my plan into effect, nobody on the entire planet will ever again laugh at another fart!"

Willy couldn't control his tears any longer.

Not only was he frightened, not only did he want to go home now, but he couldn't imagine a world where no one laughed at farts. What a sad and miserable world that would be.

Snot oozed down Willy's upper lip. He didn't dare suck it in or touch it, for fear that this weird, crazy clown would also declare that boogers weren't tasty.

"Those boogers look pretty tasty," Booby the Clown said, licking his puffy lips. "Mind if I eat 'em?"

Willy gulped hard, gathering all his courage.

"Only after you tell me why you captured us. Why do you care if people have heard of you? Why do you want to take over the world? And why, oh why, oh why, do you want to make farts not funny?"

"That's a lot of questions for one measly booger. Promise me at least one of tomorrow's batch."

"Deal," Willy said.

Booby the Clown finally released his grip on Willy's chin. He even pulled out Peter's cork. Then he returned to his throne.

"Here's my tale. *Hoo hee ha ha walla walla wing ding!* Prepare to weep!"

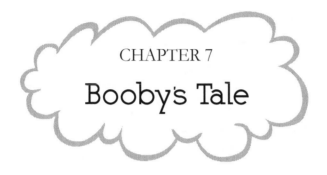

CHAPTER 7

Booby's Tale

"When I was growing up as a young clown, my parents pressured me with ridiculous expectations. You know what that's like, right?"

Willy and Peter nodded.

Their parents expected them to always wash hands after using the toilet, to tuck in shirts, eat kale salads, not retch when Aunt Bertha kissed them, and to even–*get this!*–tidy their own room on weekends. They knew what unrealistic parental expectations were like.

"I come from a long line of clowns," Booby the Clown said, "dating back to the Circus Maximus in ancient Rome. Even before I knew how to silly-walk or honk a bicycle horn, my parents told me: 'You're going to be the funniest, most famous clown in the whole world.' And they expected it!"

Booby shifted in his plastic seat, making a noise like a One-Cheek Squealie. Willy bit back a chuckle.

"I was three when they got me my first squeezy nose. They piled me with books about famous clowns and hired tutors to teach me unicycle riding and how to trip and fall funny. I was never allowed to clean up or do chores; they demanded I just play-play-play all the time.

"They forced me to read comic books and watch cartoons. Worst of all, they expected me to always burp and snort at the dinner table, and they only ever served hot dogs, and we had to squirt mustard and throw whip cream pies in each other's faces. Yes, you're lucky you don't have clown parents."

Willy tried to look sympathetic, but it actually sounded kind of good to him.

"I was sent to the best private clown school in the country. I goofed off harder than any other student, and came out top of my class. I gave the graduation speech, which was a ten-minute-long uninterrupted belch. I got a standing ovation!

"I thought my parents would be so proud. But it still wasn't good enough for them. No no no. Nothing was ever good enough. Know what I mean?" Booby buried his face in his hands.

Willy and Peter blinked at each other. Then Peter said, "Uh, yeah. We know exactly what it's like to squirt mustard and throw pies at, like, your sister, and goofing off and belching in school, and your parents for some reason acting like they're ashamed of you."

"You understand!" Booby happily honked his red rubber nose.

"I found work with the most famous circus in the country. My first performance was at the greatest show of the year, under the biggest big top. All the big clown superstars were there— Doozie and Dollie and Binky Winky and Honeypop.

"Drums rolled. Tubas blasted. I rolled out on my unicycle, juggling goldfish and teapots, then bumped into an elephant's big fat butt, exactly as I'd practiced, month after month."

Booby shut his eyes and wiped away a pretend tear.

"Then what?" Willy said.

Booby squeaked like a sad little mouse. "Nobody laughed."

"Oh," Willy and Peter said together.

"Nobody ever laughed. Not at anything I did. I played all the classic skits: kick-in-the-pants leapfrog, musical saws, soccer with dogs. Day after day, in big cities and country towns. Never got a single laugh.

"Kids tossed popcorn boxes at me. Grownups threw bottles. The ringmaster gave me one last chance.

"That night, I was doing the greasy rope climb with another clown. Nobody was laughing, as usual. I'd eaten some stale burritos that afternoon. In the middle of the act, halfway up the rope, I accidentally let out this humongous, loud, greasy fart right in the other clown's face.

"The audience laughed so loud, I fell off the rope right on the other clown's head just as another fart blasted out. The crowd went wild. Hey, don't laugh!!"

Willy and Peter clapped their hands over each other's mouths.

"They changed my name to Chucklebutt. They made me turn my whole act into fart gags. I even played tunes with my butt. All the artful and creative routines I'd spent a lifetime perfecting—all worthless.

"My entire career, my identity—*my whole life*—became nothing but a bunch of stupid fart jokes.

"When people saw me on the street they'd plug their noses and chuckle. You have no idea the humiliation I felt. I'm an artist, not a fartist! I said, don't laugh!!"

Peter held back a snicker. But Willy was starting to feel sorry for Booby.

"One day I plotted my revenge. During the lion tamer's act, while the lions and tigers were leaping through a burning hoop, I somersaulted into the center ring.

"I'd been saving up a fart all morning and let it roar. It caught fire like a blowtorch.

"The audience laughed and laughed... until the tent pole went up in flames. Luckily, everyone escaped unharmed, including the lions and tigers, who disappeared into the hills. Naturally, I was fired."

Willy felt so sad for the people, the animals, and for Booby losing his job, his lips started to tremble.

Booby stood up and paced with hands behind his back. "I wandered the country, but I couldn't even get a birthday party gig tying balloon animals. All people wanted from me was farts, farts, and more farts!"

"But what's wrong with that?" Peter said. "If people think it's funny, then that's what you should do."

Booby spun on his heels. "Wrong! *Wrong wrong wrong!* People don't recognize true genius! I am a clown of the highest pedigree and world-class comic achievement. Farting is ordinary. Farting is cheap and ugly! It produces no sense of wonder, requires no wit. Do you understand yet?"

Willy couldn't hold back his tears anymore. Booby's story was just too sad.

"No crying! I can't stand crying!" Booby yelled. "Only laughing is allowed! And I, the great Booby the Clown, will have the last laugh.

"Here on Wize Krakker Island I've devised a plan so grand, so clever, so utterly...stinky! When I am through, no one will ever again think farts are funny.

The entire world will laugh only at me! At long last, I will be the funniest, most famous clown in the whole world! *Hoo hee ha ha walla walla wing ding!*"

Willy reared back in terror as Booby leaned toward him and stretched a long, gnarly finger.

"And now for that yummy booger."

CHAPTER 8
The Labs

Booby the Clown snapped his snot-slippery fingers.

Clown guards wearing garbage pail helmets rushed into the room and hauled Willy and Peter down a long staircase chopped into the mountain rock.

Willy cried out loud. He wanted to go home.

"He's wacko," Peter said. "People have laughed at farts for millions of years. I'll bet even dinosaurs laughed at their own paleo-gassers. I don't see how he can ever make people stop thinking farts are funny."

"That's what you're about to find out," said the tough blue-haired clown whose blue-gloved fist grabbed Peter's hair.

He shoved them into a zebra-striped laboratory filled with dozens of cages and clowns in zebra-striped coats. Some held clipboards, others shoveled brussels sprouts and pickled onions through the cage bars.

Willy stepped over to see which circus animals were in the cages. He couldn't believe his eyes.

Inside, a boy around Willy's age, with dark skin and curly hair, knelt on the floor. "Eat!" a zebra clown shouted. The boy put a pickled onion and brussels sprout in his mouth. "Swallow!" the clown ordered.

"What's going on here?" Peter said.

The food clown moved to the next cage and said, "This is the FLATULAB, the Fart Letting and Tooting Underground Laboratory."

"You mean you *want* kids to fart?" Peter said. "But—"

"*Butt.* That's funny. Never say it again," the clown said. "Here's where we test different food combinations for maximum gas production."

Strange, for a windowless room where boys were forced to fart, it was completely odor-free. A boy two cages ahead let out a real buzzsaw blower that would have put a whole classroom in stitches, yet there was no smell.

Willy discovered that the boy's backside was covered by a suction cup with a tube leading into an electronic device. A clipboard clown ran over and examined the screen.

"H$_2$S zero-one-six," the clown said.

"What's that mean?" Willy said.

"Means it stinks only above average. Have to turn up the cabbage."

A clown wearing tiger stripes grabbed Peter by the neck and led him alone to a tiger-striped door.

"No!" Willy shouted.

Peter put on a brave face and winked back at Willy, but the way he squirmed and grunted, he must have been scared.

Or maybe he just had to pee. The tiger-striped clown shoved him in and slammed the door.

Then the clown turned on Willy and growled like a tiger. "Your turn soon."

Willy decided that if his brother could show courage (or hold in his pee), so could he. He pretended to be calm.

Only then did he notice the circus music playing through speakers and the circus animal dolls dangling from the ceiling.

Nothing here made sense. A fart-hating clown studying farts with clown scientists? Boys in cages—how did they get here? And more important, how would he and Peter escape?

Peter came out wearing a silly grin. Before they could exchange a word, Willy was pushed through the door. Inside a small white room, a clown dressed like some silly circus doctor grabbed him and pressed a red toy stethoscope to his chest. Willy was too scared to move.

The doctor shoved something in Willy's mouth which tasted like a cross between dog food and spray-on cheese. He wanted to vomit, but the doctor slapped his back and, without thinking, Willy swallowed.

His guts rumbled and bubbled and fizzed. Uh oh—a fart was brewing. Should he hold it in? The doctor listened with his stethoscope, then turned Willy around and leaned his face into Willy's butt.

You mean a grown-up actually wants me to fart in his face? Willy thought. *I could get used to this!*

He spread his feet just the right amount, bent one knee just so, and let out a soaring musical fart like a cow playing the trombone, right in the clown doctor's face. Now, *that* was funny, though he didn't dare laugh.

The clown doctor sat up, neither laughing nor disgusted. He tapped Willy's belly and scribbled some notes.

Then the doctor opened the door and led Willy outside.

The tough blue-haired guard clown had returned. "So? Which one you keeping?" he said.

"No!" Willy said. "You can't separate us!"

"Yeah! No way!" Peter said. "Let us go!"

"I can't use either," the clown doctor said. "These two are highly advanced farters. Not appropriate for such elementary experiments."

"Can we go home, then?" Peter said.

Willy added, "It's our sister's birthday, and—"

"Quiet!" The blue hair clown grunted. "Come along!"

They went down another rock staircase, then stopped at a door labeled: *P.U. Lab.*

A clown wearing a bowtie and gas mask motioned them inside. It was just like the FLATULAB, with one huge difference: it smelled like a thousand clogged portable potties that hadn't been emptied since the Stone Age. More cages held more boys: older ones farting and younger ones inhaling them. Here they tested the physical effects of breathing in farts.

"Where do all these boys come from?" Willy said.

The bowtied clown lowered his gas mask. "Weren't you sent here?"

"Of course not," Peter said. "We came on our own."

The clown's bowtie spun and his eyes went wide. "Never heard that one before. As for these guys, we have deals with schools. You know when a boy farts or pulls a girl's hair or says rude words in class and the teacher sends him out of the room? Well, guess where they end up?"

He rolled his eyes and laughed a goofy clown laugh.

"What about girls?" Willy said.

"What about them?" the clown said.

"Girls don't fart."

"Yes, they do," Willy said.

"Well, if they farted—which they don't—their farts wouldn't stink."

"Girl farts smell worse," Willy said.

"Hey, who's the fart expert here?" the clown said.

"Actually..." Peter began to say, but Willy silenced him with a little kick in the leg. They should be as useless as possible, so they'd be released.

"Actually, we have enough stinky farters in this lab," the bowtied clown said. "We don't need boys who also fart out their mouths. Good day."

Down a deeper staircase, this time to the Propulsive Flatulence Formation Terminal, or PFFT. Instead of cages, boys were chained inside wind tunnels, where farts were tested for speed and power.

One boy actually launched a bowling ball halfway across the room. Willy had to admit that he was impressed.

He and Peter were forced to eat greasy onion rings and prune ice cream, which tasted as gross as it sounds. Then a clown wearing a goofy sports cap and coach's whistle led them to a basketball hoop and told them to bend over. He carefully balanced basketballs on their bottoms.

"This is almost cool," Peter said. "Watch me poot a basket!" But one look from Willy reminded him: they had to try their best to be thrown out of this place.

The clown coach blew his whistle. Putting all his years of farting experience to the test, Willy tooted just enough that the basketball lifted into the air.

Peter couldn't resist showing off. His basketball rode a greenish gas stream, circling Willy's ball in a figure-eight. Not to be outdone, Willy twisted his butt muscles and made his basketball perform a loop-de-loop. The balls smacked into each other and arced through the air, dropping one-by-one into the basket.

Willy panicked. They'd lost their heads, and now they'd lose their freedom.

The clown coach grabbed them both, but instead of chaining them with the other boys, he carried them to a heavy steel door. Willy kicked and screamed and grabbed the clown's whistle, ready to blow it in his ear, until the taste of gooey thick clown saliva made him retch.

The coach pressed a big red buzzer beside the door.

A motor cranked. Gears rattled.

The door rumbled aside, revealing an inner chamber filled with flashing lights and huge monitors. But no caged boys. Just blue-haired clowns in blue uniforms, and one familiar tattooed face.

"Hoo hee ha ha walla walla wing ding! We meet again. It appears that you are the Chosen Ones I've been waiting for!"

CHAPTER 9

Fart ABC

"It's my lucky day!" Booby the Clown paced the room, hands waving as he spoke. "I had a strong sense about you boys when I first laid eyes on you. Or should I say, I had a strong *stench. Hoo hee ha ha walla walla wing ding!*"

Dozens of clown laughs echoed around the small room. Willy waited for Peter to say something, but for once he looked more scared than Willy.

"I don't get it," Willy finally said. "If

you hate farts so much, then why is this whole mountain set up as one big fart science project?"

He could have sworn that Booby hissed at him. "Have you not figured it out by now? What are you, a poo-for-brains? *Hoo hee ha ha walla walla wing ding!*"

The other clowns, laughing louder than before, circled around Willy and Peter.

Booby squatted in front of Willy and flashed his multi-colored grin.

"This is the control room for our four-part—or shall I say four-*fart*—plan to take over the world. All that research you saw going on above you? In here we put it all together, to produce military weapon-grade farts.

"Once we unleash these lethally rude bombardments upon the world, then forever after, all of humankind will associate farts with misery and destruction. No one will ever, ever laugh at a fart again."

"Oh yeah?" Willy said. "There's a problem with your stupid plan. People might not like your fart bombs, but plain farts will always be funny. So as long as ordinary folks go on making honkers and bubblers and rump rippers and tushie trumpets–"

"Don't forget fanny flappers and butt bazookas and wallpaper peelers," Peter added.

"Yeah," Willy said. "No one will ever stop laughing at farts!"

"Enough!" Booby twisted Willy's nose until it hurt. "You think I didn't take that into consideration? Part–shall I say *Fart*–B of our strategy is to eliminate mankind's ability to fart...forever!

"You may recall the exploding onion dip factory? That was only the beginning, gentlemen. As we speak, our agents are dropping gas relief pills into public water supplies all over the earth."

Booby let go of Willy's nose, licked his fingers clean, then pinched Peter's shoulder until he squirmed.

"Ah, but that's not all, my fart-tastic young friends. Turn your eyes to monitor 18 and witness Fart C!"

A screen came to life on one side of the room. A big city full of tall buildings in the background; in front was a giant green figure.

It was New York! The Statue of Liberty!

A crowd surrounded the base of the statue, all dressed in wild colors. The camera zoomed in: they were clowns! They all bent over and pulled down their pants.

The speakers roared with a tremendous buzz like a thousand power lawnmowers.

The mass fart went on and on until the statue was hidden inside a thick green cloud.

Willy heard screams.

Then silence.

The screen gradually cleared. Lady Liberty dropped her torch and plugged her nose. Then the whole statue toppled backwards into the Hudson River.

The clowns around Willy and Peter danced and played toy cymbals and kazoos and bicycle horns. All except Booby the Clown, who studied the screen, hands clasped behind his back.

"Monitor 26!" he announced.

Everyone faced the other side of the room. The Eiffel Tower stood grandly under a blue Paris sky.

A huge troupe of clowns ran into the scene. Tourists cheered, expecting a funny show.

The clowns ate something that looked like food from the PFFT Lab. Then they split into four groups and grabbed hold of the tower's legs.

Someone yelled a countdown:

"Three...two...one...*blast off!*"

A roar like a million honking geese. Greenish smoke clouds billowed around each leg of the tower.

The Eiffel Tower shook violently, then left the ground, propelled by colorful blasts of clown fart. Up it went, rocketing into the sky, until it was nothing but a tiny speck.

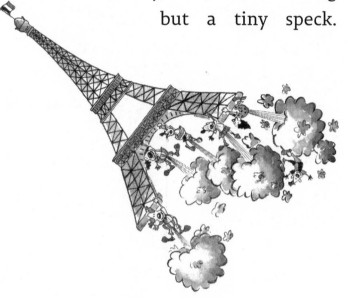

And so it continued.

A thousand farting clowns blew down the Great Wall of China.

The Sphinx of Egypt was covered in fart clouds so corrosive, it dissolved before the world's eyes.

Willy cried his guts out. He wiped his face with the back of his hand, spreading sticky snot all over his cheeks.

"Ah, more boogers. Yum yum!" said Booby the Clown, removing his glove.

"You can't have them!" Willy shouted. "You have to stop all this! Shut this down! And you have to let us go home in time for our sister's birthday!"

"That's a lot of orders in return for a single booger," said Booby.

Hulking blue clowns grabbed Willy and Peter by their collars.

"You've seen nothing yet," Booby said. "All this mischief is, shall we say, a jolly good show. But it's nothing compared to Fart D.

"And that, my feisty fart-master fellows, is where you come in."

CHAPTER 10
Fart D

Beefy gloved hands carried Willy into a cold, windowless chamber with solid rock walls.

The clown guard pressed him into a chair with a big hole in the seat like a trainer potty, and handcuffed him to the armrests.

Willy couldn't wipe away his tears and couldn't see Peter, though he heard his brother putting up a fight like an angry cat.

Why can't I be brave like my brother? Willy thought. *Why am I such a crybaby?*

"Quit blubbering," Peter said. "I'm right behind you."

Willy gulped back his crying. Indeed, they sat back-to-back in the center of the room, surrounded by clowns with big red painted-on frowns. At the end of the room Willy saw what looked like giant flying bombs with long fat hoses attached.

The guards stood to attention as Booby the Clown marched into the room. He stopped beside Willy and Peter, and pinched their chins.

"All settled in? Good. Time for science lessons," he said. "If an average person farted non-stop for six years and nine months, the total gas would have the same power as one atomic bomb. Well, guess what?"

The hand wrenched Willy's head the other direction. On the other side of the chamber was one more bomb.

"I have three, waiting to be filled with farts. What I don't have is six years and nine months. But I do have you boys, the most truly amazing fart machines I have ever seen! Using your powers of super flatulence, these warheads should be full by Monday morning. On that day I will either become supreme ruler of the entire world...or its destroyer! *Hoo hee ha ha walla walla wing ding!*"

"You're insane," Peter said. "Anyway, even we can't fart that much."

"Oh, but you're wrong, my gassy young gentlemen. Why do you think we are doing so much research? We have fabricated the finest fart-inducing food formula ever found. Combined with your, um, talents, I will reach my goal in days, not years. Let the feeding commence!"

Booby strapped on a gas mask, followed by everyone else in the room. Everyone except Willy and Peter.

A clown chef pried open Willy's jaws and spooned in a big, slimy, jiggly blob of lumpy glop. Then they clamped his mouth shut so he couldn't spit it out.

Willy gagged and choked and tried keep the goop wad away from his throat. Then he noticed something familiar, even pleasant, about its texture and flavor.

It tasted—he couldn't believe it—like an enormous, perfect snot ball.

How exquisitely gooey and squishy it felt upon his tongue. Such a delightful balance of salty-greasy flavor. Willy's stomach growled greedily. Before he could stop himself, he swallowed it whole.

"Not bad, huh?" Peter said behind him. "I'm ready for seconds."

"Yes. I mean, *no!* No way! We should be resisting them!"

"Aren't you even curious?" Peter said. "I mean, I'm against destroying the world and everything, but it'll be cool to see what kind of farts this makes."

Willy's guts began to bubble and pop, like soup boiling inside. Then his stomach swung side-to-side like a bouncing ball. From his neck down to his knees his body swelled like a balloon.

He didn't care what Peter said. He was

going to resist. He squeezed tight. He shifted on his seat. But the fumes inside him were expanding painfully. If he could just manage a one-cheek side-squeak, so the gas didn't go down the hole and into the bomb.

Behind him Peter let out a boisterous, booming bowel howl that sounded like trains colliding during a thunderstorm while marching bands played and three volcanoes went off at the same time. Willy's chair rocked in the aftershock. He couldn't hold it anymore.

He felt as if his insides were blowing out of his body. This was beyond a cheek screamer, beyond a bone rattler; this fart transported him to another dimension.

His vision turned dark, filled with green planets and yellow shooting stars. His arms turned to jelly, his legs turned to pudding. But the thing he noticed

most, the thing he didn't want to admit to himself, was this:

It was the best-feeling fart he'd ever had in his life.

Except for one.

"Psst. Peter."

"Psst. Yeah?" Peter whispered back.

"This was almost as powerful as—"

"I know."

As huge and violent as this fart had been, it was a distant second compared to the ones he and Peter had cut loose after eating camel food. In fact, he still had a handful of it in his pocket.

"We can't let them know," Willy whispered.

"Can't let me know what?" Booby's voice thundered across the room.

"Um. That...uh..." Peter stammered.

"That at this rate, you'll fill your bombs a day early," Willy said.

"That's what I like to hear," Booby said. He honked a bicycle horn. "Bring on the second course!"

The trouble was, Willy had told the truth. How were he and Peter going to get out of here and also save the world?

He had to think up a way!

CHAPTER 11

The Wee Wee Plot

The next huge snot ball was slimier and chewier than the first, and took longer to eat. The clowns had adjusted the formula, so that the farts were not so ear-splitting (though they now all wore earplugs too), but went on forever. Willy had never cut such a drawn-out, exhausting fart in his life.

"Our butts can't take this much longer," Peter said, though no clown could hear.

They were alone with three clown

minders. Willy said maybe he and Peter should talk to them. Maybe the others weren't as crazy as Booby. "Maybe they'll feel sorry for us and let us go."

"Yeah, right," Peter said. "And maybe farts don't stink."

Willy's chest heaved. It wasn't a fart trying to escape, but big, fat sobs.

Willy still blamed Peter (and their sister) for getting them into this mess, and Peter could be a big-mouthed lunkhead sometimes, but he always knew how to cheer up both of them.

Peter spoke about all the happy times they'd had together, playing pranks on the neighborhood kids.

"Remember that time we snuck up on Harry Wiener while he was taking a leak in his family's vegetable garden?"

"Yeah. We hid in the tree and farted down on him!"

Peter snorted a little laugh. "Yeah, he was so shocked that he peed all over the lettuce, and then his mother picked it for their salad!"

"Wait a minute," Willy said. "That gives me an idea."

Although the clowns had earplugs, he lowered his voice to a tiny whisper and told Peter the plan.

A pimply-faced clown slouched over and said, "Tim fer derrer diss."

"Huh?" Peter said.

The pimply clown removed his gas mask and earplugs and said, "Time for a double dose. Booby wants them bombs fully charged by midnight. Open wide."

Willy ate one snot ball, which seemed to have a slight taste of cinnamon. *Not bad,* he thought. He swallowed the next one quickly, then said, "Um, actually, I gotta go to the bathroom."

"What are you talking about? What'cha think this is?" The pimply clown pointed to their potties.

"He means we gotta take a whiz," Peter said.

The clown chef stomped over and said in a French accent, *"Ooh la la!* Zat is *eem*possible. Zis food is special formula to produce gas only!"

Willy made a big show of twisting in his seat. "Yeah, well, what about all that grape soda they gave us? You don't want us to pollute the bomb mixture, do you?"

The clown chef growled. "Why you not say so before we just feed you?" He nodded to the other clowns. "Make it *à la* speedy. We have *exactement* two minutes and forty seconds before *le* gas starts forming."

The pimply clown led them upstairs to the nearest bathroom.

"One at a time," he said.

"You realize we only have one minute twenty seconds left," Willy said.

"Whatever," the clown said. "Go together. But no monkey business!"

The boys went inside and shut the door, then gave each other a high five. They didn't really have to pee.

Just as they'd hoped, there was a small

window high above the toilet, which they were sure they could fit through, if only they could reach.

Peter stood on the seat, then Willy climbed onto his shoulders.

"If you fart now, I'll kill you," Peter said.

But Willy wasn't listening. The window was just out of reach. "Lift me up!"

Pounding rattled the door.

"Finish up, already!" the pimply clown shouted.

"Come on, come on," Peter said. "My arms are getting tired."

Willy stretched his fingers over the window ledge. With one big pull, he hoisted himself up and opened the window. He held down a hand for Peter.

The door shook on its frame. Their clown guard was trying to kick it down. "Come out, you brats!" he shouted.

Willy helped Peter up the windowsill just in time. Not only was the door coming off its hinges, but Willy's guts felt like a balloon ready to burst.

"One...two...three...*rip!!*" Peter said.

They blasted the bathroom full of a double-thick, eye-watering, poisonous fart, just as the door came crashing in.

"EEEEWWWWW!!!" said the pimply clown, right before he passed out.

Willy and Peter leapt to the ground and ran for their lives.

"Maybe we can find those camels," Peter shouted.

Trouble was, they had no idea which way to go. Ahead was open desert. Behind were jagged mountains.

"We need to head south, I think," Peter said. He pointed at the sun. "It rises in the west, right? Or east? We never decided."

Loud buzzing and whirring drowned out their voices. Something overhead blocked the light: big and round with long spinning blades, and the letters UN painted on the side.

"It's a United Nations helicopter!"

Peter shouted. "They must be searching for the secret headquarters of the Wize Krakkers who attacked all those world monuments!"

"We're saved!" Willy shed tears, but of happiness.

The boys hopped up and down, waving their arms, to get the pilot's attention.

The helicopter's deafening roar disguised the other rumbling that was happening right then, inside Willy's and Peter's bellies. Too late, Willy realized that their double dose of snotty fart food was just kicking in with part two.

Jets of gas blasted from their butts, mixing with the vomit-inducing stink still spewing from the bathroom window above, and twisted upward into the sky.

The gray-green tornado of atomic-strength flatulence engulfed the UN helicopter, which started to lose control.

"I can't look," Willy said.

"Me neither," said Peter.

They didn't have to. The next thing they heard was the shriek of a huge object falling from the sky, then a ringing crash of metal on solid rock.

Willy peeked. Something was still up there.

A parachute, with a man dangling below.

CHAPTER 12
Phew-nited Nations

"We're really sorry," Peter told the pilot, who was currently handcuffed to a potty near Willy and Peter back inside the fart bomb lab. Now *three* bombs were being loaded with gas. The pilot had a cross-eyed grin. The toxic fart cloud must have fried his brain.

"No apologies, dudes," he said. "The food here's *great*. Reminds me of something I used to eat as a kid. I just can't put my finger on it..."

Willy was about to tell him that he probably had put his finger on it—and *in* it—when the pilot's eyes bulged and his body went stiff. His earth-shattering fart rattled the walls.

"Whoa, that felt *gooood*," the pilot said. "This is fun."

Then all three of them farted together.

It sounded like herds of elephants dancing with chainsaws. The pilot sang along: "Woop doop doowap diddly dop."

The door swung open and in marched Booby the Clown.

"It appears that you boys did me a great service in your fruitless escape attempt. I should be grateful, shouldn't I? I should be lenient. Well, we don't always do what we *should* do, do we?" Booby squeezed a flower on his chest and laughed, squirting pink lemonade in Willy's and Peter's faces.

Then he squirted the pilot. "As for our new guest, I hope you enjoy eating snot and farting all day. *Hoo hee ha ha walla walla wing ding!*"

"Pretty much describes my weekends," the pilot said.

"Silence! I'll have you know that at this very moment the United Nations is in special session, waiting to hear my demands."

A cuckoo clock watch whistled on his wrist. "Ah! Show time, gentlemen!"

Booby strode to a control panel and switched on the monitor. It filled with a live picture of a huge meeting hall. People from every country of the world waited in anticipation. It was the General Assembly of the United Nations.

Booby moved in front of a camera and puffed out his chest like he was already king of the world.

"Ladies and gentlemen, Presidents and Prime Ministers, Kings and Queens, I am Booby the Clown. I present myself today as the new ruler of Planet Earth... or I will be, when you hand over the keys to your countries to me."

Protesting voices filled the United Nations General Assembly hall. Booby

silenced them with his crazy multi-
colored grin.

"Oh, but why should you surrender power to me, you ask? I shall explain! At this very moment I am preparing the most powerful *weapons of ass destruction* ever created. Each bomb packs the punch of 45 billion farts.

"All the pine-scented air freshener on the planet won't make that go away. No, sir! Your cities will smell like poo for the next thousand years! *Hoo hee ha ha walla walla wing ding!*"

The British Prime Minister stood up with a defiant tilt to her chin. "What are your requirements?"

Willy could have sworn that for just one second, the Prime Minister squinted and her bottom shifted a teeny bit to the side. She was letting out a silent stinker... right into the face of the Emperor of Japan.

"My demands are as follows." Booby

raised a gloved finger to the camera.

"First, all gas-producing crops must be eliminated. No more beans, no more onions—"

Someone called out, "What about cucumbers?"

"Absolutely no cucumbers!" Booby declared.

He held up a second finger. "All fart jokes will be outlawed. They will be deleted from every joke book in every language. Fart gags will be spliced out of movies and cartoons. No more farting e-cards. No more viral videos of baby farts! Punishment will be ten years of hard prison labor while wearing girls' panties on your head!"

"That's madness!" Willy whispered.

Booby raised a third finger. "Farting in public, farting in schools or in churches, in pools or playgrounds or work or play—

especially if those farts are silent—will result in prison for life! Yes, I'm talking about you, Madam Prime Minister, and you, Mister President of Peru. I saw you cut one."

The President of Peru blushed bright red.

"Number four," said Booby. "Imitating farts—including underarm farts or the use of whoopee cushions—is also illegal."

A woman near the front rose to her feet, let out a silent fart, and said, "What about wee wee jokes?"

Booby nodded with a little grin.

"I'm glad you asked, Madam German Prime Minister. After careful consideration, wee wee jokes are okay."

A few people applauded.

Booby raised a fist to the camera. "My ultimate condition, which is not negotiable, is that I am declared..."

Booby clamped his lips shut. Everyone in the UN held their breath. You could have heard a mouse fart.

Booby broke the silence: "...President of Our Planet in Eternity!"

The Canadian Prime Minister raised his hand. "Hey, man, that abbreviation spells POOPIE, eh?"

Pandemonium broke out. A towering woman from an African country rose from her seat and called for silence.

"What if we refuse? What if we believe that all people deserve the freedom to fart? And the liberty to laugh at farts?"

"Fine. You want to laugh at butt gas?" Booby said. "Monday morning—*yes, tomorrow!*—you'll have the biggest laugh of your life! You will watch three cities suffocate in spectacular cream-of-mushroom clouds of smoldering stink... beginning with Beantown!"

Booby clicked off the screen.

Willy and Peter gasped. Beantown! The headquarters of the Roadapple Corporation, maker of the Death Breeze 3000!

"That's so evil! And on our sister's birthday!" Willy shouted, trying to wipe his tear-soaked cheeks on his shoulders.

Booby dabbed a crusty handkerchief on Willy's face. "Cheer up, little man. Millions will get a whiff of your power-packed poots before they perish. You'll go down in history."

Then his face turned to pure evil. "Now, get to work! Fart-two-three-four! Fart-two-three-four!"

Booby marched out of the room and shut the door.

"Whoa. That dude is cool," said the pilot.

"Got any other plans?" Peter said under his breath. "Your last one didn't work out too well."

"Shut up," Willy said.

The clown chef stuffed them with more snot balls.

They tooted.

They fweeted.

They honked.

They blorked.

Willy heard a teeny-tiny sound from the pilot's seat—not a fart, but familiar.

Peter hissed to Willy, "Did you hear what I heard?"

Willy had.

It was the bleep of an incoming text message.

CHAPTER 13
The Butt Scratcher

Peter whispered through his teeth, so no clowns could overhear: "You have a phone?"

"Yup," the pilot said, way too loud. "How else my momma gonna reach me? Got it right here in my—"

"Shh!" Peter said.

"Why, you wanna call your—"

"Fart-two-three-four! Fart-two-three-four!" Peter shouted, drowning out the dizzy-brained pilot.

His brain wasn't the only dizzy one. Willy's spun like a pinwheel. *The pilot has a phone!*

Peter read his mind. "Even if we could free our hands and get hold of it, those clowns'll grab it before we can say a word."

"I have a better idea," Willy said.

"Yeah, right. Your last one was so great."

"Shut up," Willy said.

A shadow fell over Willy. The pimply clown was back. "Whadda you gabbing about? Don't waste gas out your lips." He shoved snot balls in everyone's mouths.

Willy held his snot ball on his tongue. He had to admit he was getting bored with eating boogers, flavored or otherwise. But this one had a new purpose. He let snot dribble over his lips, and stretch down in a line way past his chin.

"Ooh, yummy!" the pilot said.

"Shh," Willy hissed out the side of his mouth. He twisted and squirmed, aiming the gooey string of slime into his shirt pocket. *Don't break,* he thought. *Please don't break.*

When he was sure it was all the way in, he started to suck.

This is quite definitely gross, he thought. Just imagining what he looked like, slurping up a yellow lumpy rope of mucus, made him want to retch. But he had to look down. And what he saw cheered him.

The card that Booby had given him back in the bouncy castle room rose from his pocket, attached to the snotty string like a hooked fish. It had a picture of a clown-headed dragon, and words which Willy memorized before sucking the card all the way into his mouth. And just in time!

"Hey, you dribbled all over your shirt," the pimply clown said. "Tsk! Now I gotta get more."

"What was that about?" Peter asked.

"You'll see."

With their voices covered by a new round of loud farting, Willy asked the pilot, "Is that, um, *device* your personal one or for work?"

"All work and no gas makes Jack a dull—" *Pfoooit!*

"Shh!" Willy said. If only this dumb pilot would get his brains unscrambled! Willy spotted a bulge in his pocket where the phone must be. What if the clowns noticed too? He had to think!

The clown chef left the laboratory to get ingredients. Perfect! They only had to get rid of the other two.

"Hey, clownies!" Willy called out. "All this farting is great and all, but my butt itches bad! One of you come over here and scratch my heinie?"

"Shut it!" the pimply clown roared.

"I mean it!" Willy said. "I'm itching so bad I might let gas escape and poison us all!"

"Me too," the pilot said. "I could use a good butt scratch."

"Me three," Peter said.

The grumbling clown stomped over. "I'm just doing one of you." He reached inside Willy's pants and scratched the side of his leg.

"Higher," Willy said. "Left. No, up. Mm, that's it, right beside the hole. Ahhh!"

The clown looked disgusted. "You better not–"

But Willy did. He let out a greasy wet flapper-slapper he'd been saving up.

"EEEEWWWWWW!" The clown pulled his hand out and ran to the door. "I gotta go wash this in disinfectant!"

That left one clown, too busy at the master control panel to pay attention. No time to lose!

"Pilot man, do you have voice control on your phone?" Willy said.

The pilot replied with a bazooka-strength fart. His head rolled back, his tongue hung out. The man was useless!

Willy and Peter tried the names of all possible voice assistants, including some that didn't exist. "Natasha! Hermione! Zanzibar!"

"Zanzibar?" Peter said.

The pilot stirred. "Oh, what a fart that was. Ooh! Aah! Oh, HoneyPie!"

The faintest, tiniest mouse burp of a bleep came from the phone.

"Yes!" Willy said. "HoneyPie, send a message..."

CHAPTER 14

Celebration

Booby the Clown burst into the room, leading a parade of clowns blowing slide whistles and kazoos.

"Victory is mine!"

Booby raised his phone overhead and clicked a button.

A text message filled the largest monitor:

We unconditionally accept all your demands. You are now President of Our Planet in Eternity.

"Sure it's real?" a blue-haired clown said.

"Of course," Booby replied. "We traced the message to a United Nations registered phone!"

The other clowns cheered. "Long live POOPIE! We love POOPIE!"

"Not sure what you're talking about, but let's have a POOPIE party!" said the pilot.

Booby crouched down and patted Willy's and Peter's heads. "I couldn't call myself POOPIE without the help of your putrid powers," he said. "I hereby appoint you as ministers in my new government."

Willy put on his biggest fake happy smile, like when Aunt Bertha came to visit.

"I'm honored, Your POOPIEness. If you'll unlock us, my brother and I want to make you a big POOPIE celebration cake."

"Excellent idea," Booby said.

Willy's wrists itched after being clamped for so long. Peter pulled him aside. "What are you up to?"

"Any camel food left?"

Peter patted his pocket. A big grin spread from ear to ear. "I hate to say this, but my whiny crybaby little brother might just be a genius."

Circus music filled the air. Balloons flew everywhere. The walls were covered with signs saying, "We love POOPIE!"

While the others sang and danced, Willy and Peter worked in the kitchen. Then they decorated the cake with cherries that looked like clown noses, and carried it to the party.

Every clown on Wize Krakker Island was there. Some juggled eggs, while others did somersaults and handstands and put on magic shows.

Booby the Clown climbed onto the center table and called for quiet.

"My fellow Wize Krakkers! The great day that we all dreamed about has finally arrived. For centuries, clowns have entertained kings and queens, presidents and prime ministers, making them laugh and easing their worries. And what did we get in return? No respect! If you call someone a clown, it's meant as an insult. Well, my funny friends, the clowns' revenge has come!"

Horns tooted wildly. Crashing cymbals ripped the air.

Booby quieted them with a stern look. "New rules are now in effect," he said. "Only clowns can make the world laugh.

And what is our number one enemy in the laugh-making department?"

Every voice shouted together: "Farts!!"

"Indeed," Booby said. "As of this moment, farting is forbidden. And *laughing* at farts will never again be heard on the face of this earth."

Booby waited for the cheers to finish.

"And on that happy note..." He raised a party whistle to his mouth and blew. "Let us eat cake!"

Willy and Peter handed out slices on little party plates decorated with clowns and balloons. There was plenty for all.

The biggest slice was set on a large golden tray, which the boys presented to Booby, the new President of Our Planet in Eternity.

"Hail POOPIE!" Willy and Peter said.

"Hail POOPIE!" the clowns roared.

"Delicious!" Booby declared, wolfing

down his slice in four or five bites.

Then Booby blinked. His expression froze.

He sniffed.

"Do I smell something?"

The clowns looked at one another. Some shuffled back against the wall and held their butts. Others clamped their legs together and twisted in place.

In a far back corner, there was a little whistling hiss which ended in three bubbly pops.

Someone had farted.

A clown in the other corner turned red in the face. He covered his mouth. He tried to turn away. His knees trembled. His belly shook. But he couldn't hold it any more.

No, not a fart.

Worse.

He giggled.

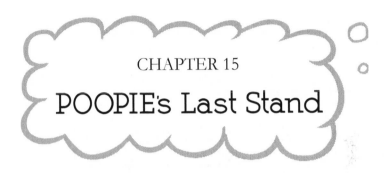

CHAPTER 15
POOPIE's Last Stand

A clown near the door let out a squealie, like a balloon releasing air. The clown beside him chuckled, just once.

"No laughing!" Booby shrieked.

But somebody else cut a rump ripper. A gulped-laugh here. A snort there.

Booby's face turned red as a fireball. "I said no giggling! No laughing! And definitely *no farting!*"

Two clowns farted at once. Even Willy joined in the laughter. But not the farts.

He and Peter had eaten no camel food cake.

By now there was no stopping the farts. Hoots and honks and toots and tweezles, gassers and wheezers of all sizes, shapes, and stinks. Blasters and bombers and zippety-doo-dahs and tushie trombones. The air turned pond scum green.

"No farting! I said, NO FARTING!!"

Booby jumped up and down on the table. But he was barely heard over the growing fart symphony: this one like a tuba, that one like a drum roll. Each new power puff caused howls of hilariousness.

"STOP LAUGHING! *STOP IT!!!*"

Booby stomped so hard that the table cracked down the middle, spilling the President of Our Planet in Eternity onto the cold, hard floor. Two clowns rushed to his side, but stopped in their tracks.

Booby's eyes bulged like they might

pop out of his head. His face turned fiery red. The clowns around him backed away.

The laughter stopped at once. So did the farting, sort of. A few little peeps and hissers here and there, but most held theirs back in pure terror.

Booby's thighs clamped together. His

face turned from red to yellow to green. Even the dragon tattoo on his forehead seemed to cross its knees.

"I will not fart," he said. "You see? I'm holding it in. That's right. I absolutely, positively will not pass gas. *Oh!*"

He twisted in place.

"Farting is forbidden. *Ack!* Farting isn't funny. *Ooh-ooh-ooh-ooh-ooh!* No, I will not!"

"Let's get out of here," Willy said.

"What about him?" Peter grabbed the pilot's arm and dragged him out into the corridor. Then Peter and Willy dashed upstairs to the nearest lab.

They ran from cage to cage, yanking out bolts. "Everybody, get out of here. Run!"

Dozens of boys stampeded upstairs.

Peter and Willy ran up to the next lab, and the next, opening cages, hoping they'd all get out in time.

Luckily the entrance guards were at the party. But no one could figure out how to open the gate.

Peter pounded and kicked at the bolt. Boys battered it with their shoulders, but still it wouldn't budge.

Willy stuck his fingers between his lips and whistled. "Everybody! Turn around and bend over! On the count of three..."

A hundred rocket-powered bowel blazers together melted the heavy iron bolt. The door flew open.

Willy and Peter stood by the entrance, making sure every boy ran outside.

They found the helicopter pilot leaning against a wall playing games on his phone.

Peter propelled him outside with an enormous kick in the behind.

"Come on!" Peter shouted to Willy.

But Willy lingered inside with a hand to his ear.

Way far down inside the mountain, a strained, desperate voice echoed through the hollow corridors:

"I will not fart, I told you! *Hoo hee ha ha!* See? I am successfully holding it in. *Walla walla wing ding!* I will...*unnngh!...* not *ffff*-fart. I-I-I-I-I...*errrrrr...oooooh...* will not–"

Uh oh, thought Willy.

"Uh oh," squeaked Booby the Clown.

The explosion threw Willy off his feet.

The ground cracked. Huge clouds of gray-green dust clogged his lungs.

Willy ran through cascades of crashing, falling rocks and gravel, barely escaping being crushed by a boulder that slammed down from above.

With one big leap, he reached open ground just as the entrance caved in, blocking it forever behind tons and tons of rubble.

Willy lay on the dirt, catching his breath. He thought he heard, echoing deep from the bowels of the earth, the buzzing and tooting of passing gas, and rowdy, hysterical laughter.

He stood up and wiped the dust from his face. Peter ran over and placed his hands on Willy's shoulders.

For the first time in his life Willy saw his brother gaze down at him from a face beaming with pride.

"Dude, that camel food truly rocks," Willy said.

Peter raised his hand to trade high fives.

"So do you, brother. So do you."

CHAPTER 16
Farts in High Places

The President of the United States looked up from the papers on his desk and leaned back in his chair.

"There they are. It's a *yuge* honor, I'm telling you gentlemen! It's the *biggest, best,* most *beautiful* honor to welcome you. Believe me, it's *tremendous!* Wait, who are these kids?"

While the President's advisers explained, Willy and Peter looked at each other in disbelief.

They were actually in the White House!

What's more, they were going to be on nationwide television to receive an award from the President himself!

It was the craziest thing to happen during the craziest day in their lives.

After being flown to Washington they'd gone straight to the Pentagon, into the secretest of top secret rooms. There they told a gathering of Generals and Admirals all the details about Booby the Clown's nuclear fart bomb.

Peter drew pictures of the whole operation. Meanwhile, Willy told them the recipe for atomic snot balls, but explained that camel food was stronger.

For their services in breaking wind for their country and the world, Peter and Willy were both made Honorary Generals in the Air Force.

Camel food was delivered from the Washington Zoo, then a general ordered a whole platoon of soldiers to test it. Luckily, Willy and Peter got out of there before the experiment began.

Even more exciting was meeting the Chairman of Roadapple Corporation. When he'd heard their story on the news, he'd hopped the next flight from Beantown, and presented Willy and Peter with the Special Gold-Plated Limited Edition Executive Pro Model Death Breeze 3000+ whoopee cushion.

Then he'd taken them to lunch in the fanciest, snootiest restaurant in the whole city, where the three of them feasted on beans and cabbage and onions. They sat there competing over who could cut the grimiest, grossest, butt-splitting howler.

The Chairman cut one so long and blubbery-sounding that half the other diners ran out screaming. Then he'd laughed and laughed. The Chairman of Roadapple Corporation was just a big kid at heart. He was cool!

And now here they were, inside the Oval Office shaking the hand of the President, while cameras flashed and reporters shouted questions.

"You boys need a drink?" the President said. Both shook their heads. The President took a sip of water—at least it was clear like water, though it smelled like something different—then covered his mouth and burped.

Whoa, Willy thought. *Wish I'd recorded that: the President of the USA's belch.*

A woman came over and fixed the President's hair, then ran a comb through Willy's and Peter's.

The President asked, "So, what'd you guys say you did?"

"We overthrew the POOPIE," Peter replied.

"Right. Where'd this happen again?"

"In a deep cavern," Peter said.

"And how'd you accomplish this deed?"

"With, um, intestinal gas, sir."

The President scratched his chin. "Okay. So, you farted and dumped a big POOPIE down the hole."

The director interrupted: "I think we're ready, Mister President."

Willy had never been so nervous in his life. The whole country—the whole world—was about to see him on television. His stomach gurgled. Deep down inside was an oh-so-familiar gaseous feeling. That lunch with the Roadapple chairman was still at work.

He squatted down low, hoping to discreetly let it out, when something caught his eye beneath the President's desk. Somebody was under there—a girl! She must be the President's granddaughter.

She was combing the bright yellow hair of an orange My Cutie Horsie. It had a gold saddle with a name, probably hers, engraved on it.

She peeked at Willy. "I heard it's your sister's birthday today."

Willy's jaw dropped when she reached over and offered him the horsie.

The director counted out loud: "Three...two..."

Willy slipped the pony in his pocket and stood up. He'd forgotten to thank the girl. Or let out his fart.

The President sniffed, and spoke to the camera:

"My fellow Americans, these brave young men served their country and the world with true distinction—and I do mean dis-*stink*-tion. I'm funny, right? Ha ha. Thanks to their courage and sharp thinking, they flushed out the POOPIE and saved us all from a smelly end. I mean, these guys are smart, which rhymes with...raspberry tart. Ha ha. I'm funny, right?"

Willy found it hard to smile for the camera. His butt was ready to burst.

The President picked up a gold medal on a colorful ribbon. "It is therefore with huge pleasure that I award to—"

PFFLO-O-O-ORRRRKK~PT~PT~PT~!

Willy held his hand over his mouth. That was Peter, not him.

People clamped their mouths shut. Except the Vice-President, who dropped against the wall laughing like a mule.

The President tried picking up where he left off.

"It is with enormous pleasure that I award to these young men—"

ffFFFF-PA-THORRRRT!

Okay, this time it was Willy. And this time no one held back. The Chief Justice of the Supreme Court spun in circles laughing, his black robe rising until you could see his undies. The First Lady dropped to the floor, laughing so hard she rolled herself into a carpet.

Only the President was unamused. "Forget the dumb speech," he said. "Guys, come get your Presidential Medal of Freedom."

Peter stepped forward and let the President place the medal around his neck. Peter held it up to the camera and kissed it. People applauded.

While Willy was getting his medal, Peter snuck behind the President's desk with that up-to-no-good look on his face.

Willy could see why. Peter had just placed the Special Gold-Plated Limited Edition Executive Pro Model Death Breeze 3000+ on the President's chair.

Willy showed his medal to the cameras, while thinking, *Please don't sit down, Mister President.*

The President sat down.

PFFFFFFLLLLLLLTHWUPPPPPP!

BLOOOOORTT!

People froze. People gasped.

The President's lips stuck out, his eyebrows squeezed together, his face turned the color of a barbecued hot dog. "Oh yeah? You think that's so funny?"

Willy gulped. Peter gulped louder. In fact, half the people in the room were gulping. It sounded like a field of frogs.

"I'll show you funny," the President, waving the TV crew closer.

Then he bent over, aimed his butt straight at the camera, and let out the most monstrous, razzle-dazzle, rancid, raging honker ever to be seen, heard, or smelled in the history of the White House.

The entire country shook so hard with laughter that later, people reported cracks along the Canadian border.

RASSP!

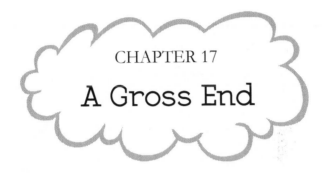

CHAPTER 17

A Gross End

Willy and Peter arrived home just in time for birthday cake.

All of Skyler's annoying little kindergarten friends were gathered around her in some girlie birthday party game.

"Ooh, there's those farty boys," said one of the friends.

"Where were you? You almost missed the party," Skyler whined.

"Didn't you see us on TV?" Peter said.

Skyler looked at her friends. They all shrugged. "I guess we were too busy playing pin the tail on the donkey."

Peter told her all about their looking for a present for her, and being kicked off a plane and sailing to a desert island where they were held prisoner by evil clowns who forced them to eat snot and fart all day.

"Ew, that's gross," Skyler said. Willy wasn't sure she believed them, but he finished the story:

"So we used camel food to escape, and we were made generals at the Pentagon and then the President gave us medals and let out a mega-supreme fart right on TV."

"Ew, that's *really* gross," Skyler said.

"But here's the best part," Peter said. "We got you the most special birthday present in the world."

He handed her a box wrapped in red, white, and blue paper that said "White House" all over it. Skyler licked frosting off her fingers and tore off the wrapping paper in big chunks.

She wrinkled her nose at the gold-plated Death Breeze 3000+. "What the−?"

"It's not just any whoopee cushion," Peter said. "See those dents? That's the butt impression of the President of the United States. For real! How many of your friends can say they have an original copy of the President's butt crack?"

Skyler's lower lip stuck out so far a plane could have landed on it. Her eyes filled with tears. "Gross!! You're the worst brothers in the whole wide world!"

Willy punched Peter in the ribs. "Told you, you stupid idiot! Should have just gotten her one of these in the first place!"

He pulled the My Cutie Horsie from his pocket "Here. The President's granddaughter gave it to me to give you. That's her name on the saddle."

Skyler cradled the precious pony in her little hands, her mouth opened so wide a truck could have driven through it. She ran to her brothers and trapped them in a tight, squeezy, squirmy hug.

"You're the best brothers in the whole wide world!"

Before they could escape, Skyler gave them each a big, wet, slurpy kiss.

"Ewwww!" Willy and Peter wiped their faces and said, "Now, *that's* gross!"

BONUS SECTION

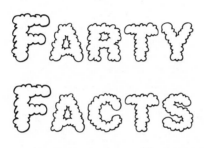

FARTY
FACTS

for curious minds

Fly the Farty Skies

People fart more while flying.

The reduced air pressure in airplane cabins makes gases expand. Which includes the gas in your intestines. Your farts can increase by thirty percent!

Farting is safest if you're flying in economy class. The fabric seat covers absorb up to half of a fart's smell. First class leather seats don't offer this advantage.

Anyway, most people aboard aren't holding it in. By the time you've crossed the country, you've breathed in the equivalent of about 200 farts.

In other words, that turbulence you feel might be coming from *inside* the plane!

Fartiest Animals

Which animal is the top farter on earth?

You might guess it's your dog. Maybe you've heard that cow farts cause global warming. But by far the fartingest animal of them all is...

TERMITES

They may be tiny, but for their body size, they fart way more than us. And there are lots of them. All the termites in the world out-fart all the humans in the world by five-to-one!

The next most flatulent creatures are:

CAMELS · ZEBRAS · SHEEP · COWS · ELEPHANTS · DOGS (fartiest breeds: Labradors and Retrievers)

Humans rate somewhere below dogs.

Maybe we should be eating dog kibble!

Fartiest Foods

What are the gassiest foods besides beans? Here's a musical menu:

METHANE-MAKING MEAT
beef, especially when cooked rare

VENTING VEGETABLES
asparagus, brussels sprouts, broccoli, cabbage, onions, artichokes, peas, celery, sweet potatoes

TOOTY FRUITS
watermelons, blackberries, prunes, apples, mangoes, peaches, pears

GASSY GRAINS
barley, rye, wheat, flax seed

CUTTIN'-THE-CHEESE DAIRY
ice cream, buttermilk, cream cheese, ricotta cheese

DUCK-QUACKING DRINKS
sugary drinks, fruit juices, beer

Forbidden Farts

Can farting really be made illegal? It already is!

In the African country of Malawi, if you break wind, you're breaking the law.

The 2011 Malawi Air Fouling Law makes it illegal to fart in public, both indoors and outdoors, even while walking down the street.

The country's Minister of Justice advised people who don't want to be arrested: "Just go to the toilet when you feel like farting."

Pity the police who have to collect the evidence.

Gas Warfare

Many online sources claim that if you fart non-stop, day and night, for six years and nine months, you produce the same amount of explosive energy as an atomic bomb.

Sadly, this isn't true.

That quantity of intestinal gas, ignited all at once, would produce a fireball over 6 miles (10 kilometers) high. Which is still a lot less than the smallest atomic bomb.

However, it *is* true that it would take only nine farts from every person on earth to produce the same power as a hydrogen bomb.

Let's all hope that there's never a World War Phew.

Who writes this stuff?

M.D. WHALEN (writer)

He was always the kid who sat in the back of the class scribbling stories and cartoons. Later he sat in front of the class scribbling stories, when he should have been teaching! Now he writes full time in the back of his house, and has published many books under other names. He also enjoys cycling, world travel, and making rude noises in different languages.

DES CAMPBELL (artist)

Brought up on British comics—Beano, Whizzer & Chips and such—Des has always drawn daft cartoons. He tries to be sophisticated and cultured, but it's all big noses, wonky teeth and funny feet... that's also how his characters look!

You are invited to
become a member of

FARTY FARTERS CLUB*

Have a *blast* with:

🌸 Free stories!
🌸 Free images!
🌸 Free sound effects! *(you know what*
    sounds we're talking about)
🌸 News about new books!

Catch a whiff at:

WWW.FARTBOYS.COM

Have you read them all?

Willy and Peter blast their way into space. But do they have enough gas in their guts to repel an alien invasion from Uranus?

Made in the USA
Columbia, SC
06 October 2017